The Mysteries of Life

By Efstratios Papanagiotou

Illustrations by Eugenia Aggelakopoulou

Followed by

Conscious Love

A Metaphysical Script

By

Efstratios Papanagiotou

Table of Contents

The Mysteries of Life

Prologue

The grandson asks; the grandfather answers. Yet, not in order to solve the questions of his young grandson but in order to expand them.

Instead of giving him easy and cliché answers which will inhibit any essential search for the meaning of life, he wants to teach him how to think, to feel and to deepen in the existential questions that trouble every child.

So in this short story the grandfather and his grandson try together to penetrate into the Mysteries of Life.

1

It was a sad day. Or at least that was what everybody said, because he didn't feel that way. He was joyful as yesterday, not in the same way though, because his joy seemed to struggle with the sadness around him.

They said that uncle N. had died. But why everyone was so sad? What did it really mean that uncle N. had died? That he slept, as someone said, or that he "left" as many people were saying?

He could not understand; but what impressed him most, was the sadness… so much sadness… struggling with his joy…

"Go outside to play" they told him.

He went outside but the mood for playing was gone; even if sadness hadn't overcome his joy, curiosity had… So many words that seemed important, "death", "funeral", "cancer"… And when he tried to understand what really happened, he received some incomprehensible answers. "Heaven", "paradise", "God", were some of the words he heard, which he had heard before, but he wasn't so sure what exactly did they mean…

"Grandpa will explain to me" he thought. His grandfather was always willing to spend time with him, a lot of time, in order to explain him the Mysteries of Life; the name he had given to his grandson's questions.

Once he had asked him, "Grandpa, what is God?" and his grandfather had answered with a serious smile, "Ah! So you want to know the Mysteries of Life!"

"The Mysteries of Life" he repeated in wonder and awe… yes, he liked that… "The Mysteries of Life"…

"Yes, I want to know them" he had said with enthusiasm and impatience.

"Hmm… "What is God?:… hmm… this is difficult… I need time to answer you… do you have time?"

He didn't like this… yes, he had time, but he didn't want to wait, he wanted to know now!

"Yes, I have" he had answered unwillingly.

But his grandfather didn't eventually answer him, "What is God?"

He had started instead asking him questions:

"Do you love your parents?"

"Yes" he said willingly.

"A lot?"

"A lot!"

"Why do you love them?" his grandfather had asked him.

"Because they love me", he had said without much thought.

"Hmm… that's the way it is; if someone truly loves us, it's difficult not to love him back."

That day he hadn't learnt anything about the Mysteries of Life. His grandfather had asked him about school, his friends and many other things, but not a word about "What is God?"

He said he needed time to answer him. Himself, on the other hand, despite the fact that he had said that he had time, he was not so willing to wait… he would ask elsewhere!

Yet, his grandfather was unique… and he loved him a lot. He always told him, "My child's child is twice my child!" And his grandfather seemed to know everything; so he wasn't impressed when after some time, and specifically in that day of sadness, his grandfather asked him: "Did you learn what God is?" as if he knew that his grandson wouldn't be patient and was going to ask elsewhere as well.

"No" he answered a little bit disappointed, since even though he had received some answers, he hadn't really understood them.

"You know that you are twice my child, don't you?" his grandfather told him, changing once again the subject.

"Yes" he nodded.

"Since you are the child of my child", he said meaningfully and asked him gracefully: "Do you have any children?"

"No!" the small kid answered laughingly.

"Will you have children?"

"I don't know", he shrugged.

"Ah! Children are God's blessing!" said his grandfather in a serious tone.

"There comes God again!" he thought, "but what is God?" he pondered, without daring to ask, since his grandfather might start again with *his* questions.

Nevertheless, it wasn't easy to avoid them.

"So you didn't yet learn what God is?"

"No", he answered expectantly.

"You might be the youngest in your family but since you want to know about the Mysteries of Life, it seems you're not so small, are you?"

"No, I am not", he said confidently, since that was true; even if he was the youngest one, he didn't feel so small; especially as small as his oldest siblings said he was…

"But do you know why your parents have so many children?"

They were indeed a big family, one more brother and three sisters.

"Because they love us!" he said after a little thinking, remembering how many times he had heard his mother telling them how much she loved them.

"Bravo, my child! And which one do they love the most?" his grandfather asked him seriously.

"All the same!" he answered confidently, as he had been taught to say, but also because he felt that way.

"Bravo, my child! That's the way it is, true love cannot be measured…" said his grandfather, again in a serious tone.

"So your parents love you and brought you in this world out of love, is that so?"

"Yes" he nodded equally serious.

"In the same way, your grandma and I had children out of love, and you also, if you ever have children, it will be out of love, wouldn't it?"

"Yes", he said feeling however that having children was not one of his concerns.

"So God created us out of love as well" said his grandfather rather indifferently.

"Hey!" felt the small child; that interested him!

"God loves us, grandpa?" he asked with interest.

"God, my child, is full of Love" said his grandfather in a profound way.

"And how did God create us?" he asked with evident interest.

"What is your favorite food?" his grandfather asked him playfully, changing completely the subject.

His young grandson had learned some of his ways, so without being bothered from the sudden change, he answered immediately:

"I like everything, but most of I like water melon!"

"And what does your mother tell you if you don't eat your food?"

"That I won't grow!"

"That is true my child… we eat to live and to grow because our food provides us with life."

His grandson pondered a little and for the first time he appreciated the food he was eating. Up to now he ate when he was hungry, because he liked it, but now he understood more clearly why he was eating and the great importance of food.

"That is the way that God created us my child; He created Nature and gave her Life, and Nature gave Life to man, she gave him his body… but then God put inside him his spirit."

"His spirit" pondered the small child.

"What is the spirit, grandpa?" he asked, though he was already tired from the new things he had learned regarding the Mysteries of Life.

"Did you love your uncle, my child?"

"I loved him grandpa, even though I didn't see him very often."

"Yes, I know my child, that's the way love is, she doesn't take into consideration this kind of things."

That day, they didn't say anything else, because this time his grandpa didn't have a lot of time; he had to be with the grown-ups. Yet, he didn't seem as sad as they did; he wasn't joyful of course, as he used to be, but he was neither sad.

He was rather more thoughtful than he was usually, and serious, very serious, bearing in mind that his grandfather always found opportunities to joke and he hardly ever lost his good mood.

But that day was different; and so they didn't say anything more, even though he wanted to ask a lot of questions. He knew however that soon he would found the chance again and that his grandpa would spend time with him, as much as it was needed… Already that day he had learned something very important, that **God is full of Love**.

16

2

Even though he really wanted to know the Mysteries of Life, he wasn't always in the mood for them. Today for example he had a fight with one of his schoolmates, a very difficult kid, as they said, who created always troubles.

So when he met with his grandfather, even though inside him he was glad, outside he looked in a very bad mood.

"Why you pretend being angry when you want to smile at me?" said his grandfather and stole him a little smile.

Yet, very quickly the small kid decided to remain faithful to his anger and frowned again.

"I am very angry" he said determinedly.

"Are you sure?... Hmm, so you're not in the mood to talk about the Mysteries of Life… You know that's better… because I…" said his grandfather and stopped as if he was pondering something.

"What?" asked his grandson, with a sudden interest.

"…you know, I am very angry as well! Some rascal treated me very rude today, and if I was just a little younger, I would teach him a lesson!" said his grandfather heatedly, raising his closed fist in the air.

Suddenly the atmosphere changed. The young kid was annoyed. He didn't like seeing his grandfather angry, although that was a very rare phenomenon. His grandfather was kind and benevolent, that's why he appreciated him so much and thought of him as a beautiful man.

But if he ever got angry, he was another man, he became more…

"Anger makes people ugly, isn't that so?" asked his grandfather smilingly as if he could read his thoughts, having suddenly changed entirely his mood.

"Yes" he replied smilingly as well, relieved that this atmosphere didn't last too long.

"But you know why do people get angry and why do they become mean?"

No, he didn't know, he hadn't ever thought about it.

"So think about it…" his grandfather urged him, but he soon interrupted his ponderings: "How was school today?" he asked with sincere interest but the small kid frowned again when he remembered his mean schoolmate.

"Not so well" he said angrily.

"Why are you angry with me?" his grandfather asked him in a sad way.

"I am not angry with you" said the kid apologetically.

"So what are you angry with?" asked his grandfather benevolently, but without waiting for an answer, he continued:

"You know, we all get angry with various things we consider mean, and even more with the people we consider mean…" he said in a serious tone, and suddenly, as if he was ready to be heated again "…like this rascal today who…" But he stopped equally suddenly, looking playfully at his worried grandson, and told him calmly "but you should know my child, that no man is really mean."

This had a real effect on him… "And all these mean people in movies, games, in the conversations he overheard, in his school… what were they? Good people?" he asked himself.

"There are no good and mean people my child… there are only happy and unhappy people" said his grandfather and stopped, giving time to his grandson to understand his words.

"There are only happy and unhappy people" his grandson repeated, continuing to wonder.

After a while his grandfather continued very seriously "The unhappier one feels, the more mean he becomes and the happier one is, the more good he is."

Yes, that was true… his grandfather was right… this mean kid in school was never really happy; he might laugh at the expense of other kids but he always seemed… sad, unhappy, he was never smiling and… bright…

The young kid was now feeling bad for having been mean to… the mean kid from his school.

His grandfather looked at him smilingly but he didn't seem willing to speak anymore. And it was true that his grandson had felt so many things in one meeting that he was calm on one hand but on the other exhausted.

Most of all though he was impressed by what he had realized; that **meanness is proportionate to unhappiness and disproportionate to happiness**.

3

Few days after the funeral of uncle N. his grandfather took him for a walk. He had promised him a "magic" surprise but the young grandson knew his grandpa pretty well, so he knew he could never know what to expect from him! When he wasn't expecting it at all, his grandfather might surprise him immensely, whilst when he had a lot of expectations from him, he was usually disappointed… to be enchanted later on when he was least expecting it!

So this time, his grandfather had promised him a "magic" surprise. He said he would show him one of the greatest Mysteries of Life, perhaps the greatest…

They went for a walk into the country, without much talking, since his grandfather was very silent and the young kid extremely enthusiastic for what was about to follow.

At some point, his grandfather stood in a certain spot. He kneeled to the ground and nodded with great gravity to his grandson to kneel as well.

"Dig with your hands a small hole here" he told him and the young child got into working with an equal gravity.

When he finished, his grandfather told him with great solemnity, "Take this little diamonds and hide them in the hole".

The young child, taking into his hands the "little diamonds", asked surprised, "What are these?" since it was obvious that the only thing that his grandfather hadn't give him, was diamonds!

"These, my child, are invaluable Seeds of Life" his grandfather answered very profoundly.

The small kid responding to the solemnity of his grandfather, without of course understanding very well what exactly they were doing, he placed carefully the "little diamonds" into the hole and covered them with some earth.

"Now pour upon them this precious liquid" said his grandfather and handed him confidentially the flask with water that they carried.

Afterwards they returned equally silent back to home. The young grandson enjoyed a lot the walk into the country and the sense of importance which accompanied it, so having been through a great day, he didn't pay much attention to the fact that he hadn't perceived that day anything unusually magical or mysterious.

From time to time they visited this place with his grandfather and poured some "precious" water to the "little diamonds" which had grown and had become marvelous green blades of grass.

The kid was taking care of them with great attention but wasn't impressed much by them. Nevertheless he was enjoying a lot these country walks.

So he was very joyful that day, when his grandfather showed up and told him to take a walk into the country.

He was joyful for two reasons: one was because he liked these walks and the other one was because he found a chance to go away from his home for awhile where this known old sadness has returned…

In his house, friends and relatives had gathered after the "memorial service" of uncle N. as they said, and he was faced again with the same questions but mostly with the question, "Why so much sadness?"

When they got to the spot where the "little diamonds" had grown after taking care of them for some time, his grandfather kneeled to the ground and with great tenderness he caressed the green blades of grass.

This gesture got the attention of the small kid who kneeled down as well, looking for the first time really carefully the green blades of grass.

They seemed to him so… magic!

They were beautiful, simple, bright, harmonious, joyful and mostly… alive!

So he was astounded when he saw his grandfather grabbing all of them softly with his big hand and with a gentle gesture cutting them all at once! The scene lasted only few seconds but was engraved in his mind… and then he felt being overwhelmed by a small sadness… "Ah, the known sadness…" he said to himself.

His grandfather asked him to dig a small hole next to the blades of grass in the same way he had done when they had to bury the "little diamonds" in order to hide them. The young child devoted diligently to his work and as soon as he finished he looked sadly at his grandfather, waiting for the next step.

His grandfather laid the little green blades of grass into the small hole and asked him to cover it with earth. When his grandson finished, he asked him solemnly:

"Do you know what will happen with the blades of grass which had grown from our "little diamonds"?

"No" waved the small kid silently, full of mixed emotions, since he really didn't know what will happen with them.

"They will return to where they came from" said his grandfather in a profound way.

The young child looked at him with awe in his eyes, since he really imagined the little blades of grass travelling back to their place of origin.

"You see my child, nothing is lost… whatever is born, grows, matures and dies, which means that it returns where it came from, to make a new beginning."

His grandson wanted to ask where do things come from, but he didn't have to, because something inside him reminded him that all comes from God, from Love.

In the way back to his home which was full of sadness, due to the memorial service of his uncle N. his grandfather turned to him seeing him sad and told him with a serious smile:

"Don't be sad, my child… because death is not but a return… for a new Beginning."

The young grandson cheered up immediately and looked at him with hope in his eyes. This had been a truly magic day for him… because he had understood that **death is not the end, it is another Beginning**.

4

His grandfather, despite his age, had a very good memory. Even though he seemed to change subjects abruptly, jumping from an issue to another, he never forgot what they said in their conversations and where they had left unfinished matters. This was due to the fact that he paid great attention to what he said and to what he was being told. So he could often reproduce with amazing accuracy conversations that his interlocutors had either distorted in their mind or had forgotten completely.

His young grandson now seemed to have "inherited" this faculty of his grandfather, at least in relation to subjects and conversations that really mattered for him. So he wasn't impressed at all when his grandfather told him:

"Do you remember when you asked me about the spirit of man?" and without waiting for his grandson's reply, he asked him seriously:

"Do you love your parents a lot, my child?"

"Yes, a lot" answered equally serious the young child, whilst he could not refrain from wondering why did his grandfather reminded him about the spirit of man, since he wasn't going to talk about it.

"Can you show me how much?" asked his grandfather with sincere interest, as if he was asking him to show a new toy of his.

His grandson hesitated for a moment since he thought of telling him "From here up to the sky" or opening widely his hands saying, "That much" as he always did, when they asked him these kind of things. But he knew that these answers always produced smiles and laughs, whilst his grandfather looked very serious, as if he was expecting to show him something very tangible. So he just waved negatively with his head and waited.

"You see my child, we cannot see love with our eyes, neither grasp it with our hands but we feel it with our heart", said his grandfather contemplatively, "there are a lot of things we cannot see but only feel".

His young grandson wasn't sure if he understood all these things his grandfather was telling him but deep inside him he felt that they were true and most of all interesting. Still though, he couldn't see what the connection of love with the spirit of man was.

"That is what happens also with God, my child…"

The small kid opened widely his eyes "…ah, God…" he thought.

"…we cannot see Him with our eyes, neither touch Him with our hands but we feel Him with our heart… with our spiritual heart… with our spirit, because God is spirit" said his grandfather and stopped abruptly.

The young child was absorbing every word. He felt confused but he was confused in the same way as when you have in front of you different pieces of a puzzle and you know that if you connect them correctly, the right image will emerge.

"So I really need time to learn about the Mysteries of Life" he pondered, but now he liked this idea because as it seemed the Mysteries of Life were much more important than he thought initially.

That day he might not learned something specific but he had really **felt** the value of **patience**.

5

"God is Love", pondered the young child, "and God is Spirit". "So Love… is perhaps… Spirit?"

"Has this any sense?" he wondered. But what else had he learned from his grandfather? That God gives man his spirit… and that man feels God with his spiritual heart… with his spirit… "Hmm… that makes some sense… God gives man his spirit so he can feel Him… since he cannot see Him nor touch Him…"

The small kid felt he was approaching to the solution of the Mystery, to the solution of the puzzle, but something was missing… "God is Love and God is Spirit, so Love is closely connected to Spirit, and God gives man his spirit… so what is the spirit of man… perhaps… perhaps it is the Love within man's heart?"… Yes!... now the image seemed more clear, as if everything was slowly getting into their place…

But he had to show the puzzle he had composed in his mind to his grandfather, and ask him what he thought of it, if it was correct…

So when they met that day, the young child explained to his grandfather what he had understood and after he finished, he asked him anxiously: "Is that so, grandpa? Our spirit, is the Love we have within our heart?"

His grandfather smiled meaningfully and answered with a question:

"Do you pray my child to God?"

The young child used to the deviations of his grandfather, answered with certainty:

"Yes, grandpa, every night!"

"Only in the night, not in the morning?"

The small kid was surprised "No…" nobody had told him that he could say his prayers in the morning as well… Quickly though he found the solution… "But every morning we say our prayer in school…" he said triumphantly.

"And afterwards?" his grandfather continued.

Now the small kid really wondered, "Afterwards?" he thought… "Afterwards?" he asked.

"Yes, afterwards… you don't pray again the whole day?" his grandfather asked very simply as if he was really wondering.

Now this was unheard of… to pray during the day… no, nobody had told him this… that it could happen… even though… sometimes… if he needed something… if something went wrong… yes, then he would say some prayer… to God… So he said hesitantly:

"Sometimes… if there is some need…"

"God, my child, is always with us, you know that?"

Yes, he had heard that… but he couldn't say that he had truly realized it himself… "Yes" he said hesitantly again.

"And you know why He is always with us?" his grandfather asked in a conspiratorial way as if he was ready to reveal some great secret.

"No" said the small kid with evident interest.

"To keep us Alive my child" his grandfather said solemnly. "Without God we could not live for a minute longer".

"Ah…" the kid thought, "so God is truly useful after all…" he pondered impressed. That was a real revelation… and enough for today… he might not have learned exactly what he was asking, but he had surely learned something very unexpected, something very important, that **God is our Life**.

6

"So could we say perhaps that *Love is our Life...*" that was the thought that awaked him in the morning, "since God is Love and God is our Life".

It was really strange but the more he learned about the Mysteries of Life, the more he realized that he didn't know anything; the more answers he received regarding them, the more questions were raised...

But today one certain question was raised within him:

"Grandpa, is Love our Life?" asked his grandfather the next time he saw him.

"Yes, my child", his grandfather gave him a certain answer, and continued, "Love is the Life within everything my child... the more love there is in anything, the more alive it is... when the Love withers, Life withers as well..."

The young grandson wasn't sure if he had understood everything. These Mysteries of Life seemed constantly to slip away from his "hands"...

"Love, my child, can take the form of a flower, of a fruit, of an animal; She can take any form, of water, fire, wind and earth. Love is One but can take many forms. And of course Love can take the form of a man and She gives Life to our spirit. Love, my child, real, pure Love is the Life of our spirit".

"But what exactly is our spirit?" the kid kept wondering, fascinated by what he was learning.

"Now, our spirit, my child, is our real self, it is what we truly are deep within us" said his grandfather as if he could read his thoughts.

"And since Love is the Life of our spirit… we could say that our real self is…" said his grandfather and paused.

"…Love" added with certainty the small child.

"Yes, my child" said with equal certainty his grandfather.

"Finally!" he thought joyfully because he managed eventually, through these certain questions and certain answers to realize that **Love is our Real Self**.

7

Yet, all these answers regarding the Mysteries of Life, had brought forth a question, an unsolved question: "If God is Love and Love is the Life who has created everything… then, who or what created God?"

That's exactly how the young grandson formulated his question to his grandfather, after much pondering, not having been able to give a certain answer to this certain question.

"God my child, creates God, as Life creates Life", said with certainty his grandfather, "and as Love bears…"

"…Love" said with certainty his grandson, remembering how he loved his parents because they loved him, and how they loved him because… he loved them…

"You see, my child, it takes time and patience to learn the *Mysteries of Love*…"

"Of Life" he was about to correct him but he stopped as soon as he reflected that Life and Love were eventually the same thing…

"So as you will grow", his grandfather continued, "you will understand all the more that **the greatest Mystery of Life is… Life Herself**".

"Or **Love**…" pondered the young child.

43

Conscious Love

A Metaphysical Script

By

Efstratios Papanagiotou

47

Dedicated to Ioanna

Prologue

This story has been written in the form of a "script" that is why it is accompanied by the according musical soundtrack. The songs that have been chosen are not by random both regarding their musical genre and their lyrical contents.

Therefore it would be rather interesting for the reader if he could combine his reading with the hearing of these specific songs (when some "scene" is accompanied by music) so this "play" can become as much live as possible in the "screen" of his mind.

The songs which are heard are the following:

Song: Jah is the way

Artist: Israel Vibration

Album: Why you so craven

Song: Time

Artist: Don Carlos

Album: Seven days a week

Song: Know your past

Artist: Morgan Heritage

Album: More teachings

Song: Wake up and live

Artist: Bob Marley and the Wailers

Album: Survival

Song: Dream

Artist: Groundation

Album: Young tree

Song: Who the cap fit

Artist: Bob Marley and the Wailers

Album: Rastaman Vibration

Song: Judge not

Artist: Morgan Heritage

Album: Three in one

Song: One more day (Live it up)

Artist: Groundation

Album: Each one teach one

Song: Is this love

Artist: Bob Marley and the Wailers

Album: Kaya

Song: Jah is the way

Artist: Israel Vibration

Album: Why you so craven

***

(Music: Jah is the Way – Israel Vibration)

In the city, two friends are walking, talking with each other, looking in a good mood.

(Music fades out)

At some point one of them turns to the other after having turned behind to look and says:

- I think someone is following us.

The other guy with an unchanged good mood replies:

- Why would be someone following us, you just imagine stuff...

The first one says more seriously this time:

- No, I'm sure someone is following us.

The other guy remains amused and turns back to look just for fun, yet in a different direction from where his friend is looking, and a little bit worried turns to him:

- You're right! There is someone following us.

His friend realizes that he didn't look where he is looking at:

- Where are you looking at? He is not from this side!

And then he looks to the place his friend is looking and sees two more guys following them:

- They're more! Now three guys following us!

The other man looks quickly to where his friend was looking and sees two guys and then looks back to where he first looked and sees now three guys:

- They're multiplying! They're five now! We must have done something very bad...

- We haven't done anything.

Both of them are looking behind them, while they accelerate their pace, and now they see almost ten people following and approaching them from all different directions.

Everyone else around them is walking normally without seeming to notice anything strange.

The two friends are now moving faster and suddenly one says to the other:

- Turn here! thinking that he knows a way to escape from them.

But now they find themselves surrounded by these guys who had regular appearances just a little while, but now they're dressed with strange clothes almost like primitives and have different faces, they look like savages now.

The two surrounded friends are almost terrified and also puzzled with the fact that nobody from the ordinary people passing them by pays any attention to them.

So without even trying to ask for help, they find themselves, very suddenly and quickly, with their legs spread and their arms raised, tied up against the wall, to some small peculiar mechanisms.

They think they're going to be tortured, so they look very anxious but at the same time amazed because all these are happening very quickly, almost in a magic way.

One of the "savages" approaches them and says, with a deep, gentle, steady voice, to the man who first saw them (protagonist named John):

- Don't be afraid, we are not going to harm you.

His voice and his manners immediately calm the two men, and the whole atmosphere of anxiety and fear disappears.

Now as if all of these are normal the other man (not John) asks:

- What do you want from us?

The strange guy, as if he hasn't heard the question, just continues his speech:

- We have a gift for you, we will give you what you've always dreamed of, we will make you capable of "seeing".

You will be able of knowing, feeling and sensing everything as it really is. You will be able to perceive *reality*.

Before they have time to respond, some of the strange people adjust very quickly in their eyes some very small and simple devices that hold their eyes a little bit more open, they still can move them but the opening around their eyes, between their eyebrows and just below their eyes, is a little wider.

They don't feel uncomfortable with these devices and one of them (John) asks:

- Why are you giving this gift to us?

- It is a gift for you, but also an expirement for us, we want to learn something from your new way of seeing.

- And how will you know what we see?

- We have our way, take advantage of this gift; it's all that you've ever wanted.

***

With a sudden move, John wakes up. He is excited, and has these small devices round his eyes but he doesn't notice them. He looks around and realizes that he is at his appartment. Almost at the same time his friend Matthew (the second man of the dream) wakes up too. They look at each other and John says:

- I saw an incredible dream, it was very strange…you were there too…some guys were following us and….

Matthew immediately gets up too:

- I saw the same thing, we were together in this dream…

They realize that they saw the same dream and stand for a while amazed, trying to remember it.

John:

- …the strange people…the small devices…it was the most realistic dream I've ever been to…eh…seen, I mean…

- John what's this around your eyes?

John reaches his eyes and realizes that the small devices are there, and carefully, not to ruin them, touches them. He is really amazed but at the same time, he feels that all these are very natural and says to Matthew:

- You have them too!

Matthew also realizes that he has round his eyes these small devices and says:

- It wasn't just a dream it really happened.

- You're right! I can sense it, I can "see"…, I feel I can understand everything…I've got to tell this to the others!

- Go ahead, I'll be waiting for you here, I have to realize what really happened.

John goes to the living room. Gently, he wakes up Luke:

- Luke, Luke, wake up, I saw an incredible dream which has turned into reality!

Luke slowly wakes up:

- Oh, I was seeing an incredible dream too,yeah I wish it was real…

and turning side to sleep again, 'it was incredible indeed…'.

John doesn't let him to go back to sleep and pulls him to his side:

- Look! Look at my eyes, what do you see?

Luke, annoyed:

- What do you want me to see?

and he looks but he doesn't notice anything particular.

- Don't you see these small devices round my eyes?

Luke, pretty amazed:

- What devices! I don't see a thing.

John stares at him:

- …I "see", I understand you're awake but in fact you're still sleeping…you just *can't see*!…

Luke, really annoyed, turns to the other side to continue his disturbed sleep:

- You're really something! How come I'm sleeping since you don't let me to, but you…you should wake up…you're still dreaming.

John lets him sleep and at the same time listens to a sound from the kitchen and goes there. He enters and finds Mark eating his breakfast. Mark looks at him a little bit indifferent:

- Good morning…what's these things on your eyes?

John gets excited:

- You see…you see them!

- Of course I see them, what are these?

- It's incredible, I saw a dream-

Mark interrupts him:

- Could you tell me about all this another time because I have to finish my breakfast and then I have some things to do.

John is puzzled:

- Are you serious?… The most amazing thing has just happened to me and you're saying you have to finish your breakfast?

Mark very naturally:

- But that's true, I have to finish my breakfast.

- We've always talked about finding something meaningful in life and now that something really extraordinary happened, you don't care to listen?

Mark while eating replies:

- You're right, come on tell me, what happened?

John ponders a little and starts:

- As I was saying I saw this dream where one guy was following me and-

Mark indifferently interrupts:

- Someone was following you?…Why?

- I was just about to tell you, please be patient and listen!

He is about to start again but Mark finishes his breakfast and he is getting ready to leave:

- You know…I think it's best if we leave it for another time, I have some things to do.

John looks thoughtful:

- Now I understand, you saw the devices on my eyes but you're not ready to listen…You're afraid to listen that what happened is just what we've always wanted, you just *don't want* to listen'.

Mark replies while leaving:

- No that's not true, I'll listen to you, but just not now, perhaps we'll talk later…ok?

***

John sits alone trying to realize what has happened, the small devices are gone from his eyes but he doesn't know it yet. Matthew enters in the kitchen:

- How did it go?

- They didn't want either to see nor listen…they're just not ready for this…but it doesn't matter, if we're capable of "seeing", we'll help them somehow and one day they'll "see" too.

Matthew rather doubtfully:

- We'll help them to see what? Maybe there is nothing to see, maybe all this was really just a dream.

- A dream that we both saw?

- It could happen, who knows how these things work? And then again it might wasn't exactly the same dream.

- And what about the devices on our eyes?

- What devices? I don't have anything on my eyes.

- Yes, indeed, you don't!

- Neither do you.

John reaches to his eyes and realizes that he hasn't anything round them.

He ponders for a moment and says:

- It doesn't matter, I'm still capable of "seeing", of understanding, these were only helpful devices, now we don't need them, now we know how it is to "see".

Matthew, relieved:

- I don't agree with anything you're saying, all this was just a dream.

John stares at him and says:

- Don't be afraid, it doesn't matter that no one believed us, you know for yourself that it wasn't just a dream.

- I'm not afraid of anything…and the only thing I know for myself is that all this was just a dream.

John says, rather to himself:

- That's why nobody wanted to listen or see, if you who had the experience of all this, you choose now to be deaf and blind, imagine the others who didn't have even the slightest idea of what we felt, of what is like to "see".

Matthew pays almost no attention to him and looks what is there for breakfast.

***

John wakes up with a sudden move, this time for real. He looks anxious but after a minute, looking around him, realizes that all this was just a dream. Quickly he gets up, looks for pen and paper to write down this strange dream, but then he realizes that all the images in his mind seem already rather distant. He puts aside the pen and paper and looks outside the window at the countryside. He is at his parents' house in a farm. Then, he looks in a bag for a Cd, he finds it, he puts it in the Cd-player.

(Music: Time – Don Carlos)

He sits again at the window looking outside. He smiles with the first lyrics of the song. He dances a little as he's getting dressed and then his brother enters. He dances a little too; they smile and hug each other.

(Music fades out)

His brother:

- When did you arrive?

- Late last night.

- Have you seen mom and dad yet?

- No, not yet, how are they? How is mom?

- It was a bit sudden for them but they knew she was old, they've taken it well, yeah… I think mom is ok.

- I expected that, mom is always strong…Ok, then everything is good…let me get ready and I'm coming down.

- Ok,…I'm very glad to see you.

- Me too…

***

He goes down to the kitchen, he sees first his mother.

His mother:

- Oh, here's my prodigal son, how are you John? How long has gone by?

He hugs her:

- Come on mom, don't start, how are you?

- I'm ok…I'm very happy you could come.

- You know I would…Hey dad, how are you?

- I'm ok…I'm happy to have you here.

- Yeah…I'm happy to be here too, he sits for breakfast.

His father:

- How is your life son?

- Fine dad, everything is fine.

His mother:

- Of course it's fine, if you don't have to work…what was this job you left?…Your seventh?

- I didn't know you were counting them mom.

- Of course I'm counting them, what was it now with this one? Why wasn't it good enough for you?

- I wasn't good enough for it! I was more than good for it! Come on mom, you know I don't want to chain myself down, I have a life to live.

- Everyone has a life to live and yet everyone is working.

- I work to live, other people live to work.

- Oh! You and your smart answers!

- You know mom that I'm content with little, I don't need to be rich, I'm not searching for material happiness.

His father:

- Ok son, but what are you searching for?

John:

- ……………..

His mother:

- Yes John, what are you searching for?

- …If I knew what I was searching for, I would have found it… I don't know… I'm searching…

Silence.

John:

- Anyway, it's always very constructive when I see you! It's always nice to be back home!

His mother:

- Oh, come on John, nobody wants to-

- I know mom, I'm just teasing you, you know I always enjoy being here.

- Yes, I know.

Everything is taking place under a good mood and a nice atmosphere, epsecially from the side of John who faces his parents with a sense of humour.

He finishes his breakfast and stands up.

His mother:

- At your brother's room, there are your clothes for the funeral, go and try them.

- Ok, mom, I will.

***

He sits on a hill at the countryside with his brother. They look at the view and discuss.

John:

- It's strange, death is the only thing that everybody dislikes and yet the only thing you can rely on.

- What do you mean "rely on"?

- I mean it is the only thing that we know beyond doubt that is going to happen to us too, we don't know anything about our future, whether we'll have an easy or difficult life, whether we'll have a wife or kids, friends or not, health, happiness, accidents, money, we don't even know what the next day will bring, not even the next hour…

- I know I'll be listening to your philosophies for the next hour…

- No, I'm talking seriously…we don't know anything about what the future will bring but we know one thing for sure, that someday we will die…

- That's not a very pleasant thing to think about…

- On the contrary, if we could realize the fact that someday we will die and not knowing when this day might be, we could live each and every day of our life more complete…more meaningful…Grandma used to tell me that the first Christians had a spiritual exercise…I think it was called "remembrance of death".

- What kind of exercise is this?

- They had to think everyday about the inevitability of their own death… I don't know… maybe in this way they wouldn't go after anything vain…

- Yeah, of course, if you remember everyday that you're going to die, everything will seem vain…

- …I don't know… I would like though, to live everyday as if it would be my last…

- So why don't you do it?

- I can't…I don't know what I would do if I had one more day to live…

Silence.

They look at the view.

***

Along with his family he attends a small funeral with a few relatives.

***

He kisses his family goodbye at the bus stop.

His mother:

- Are you sure you don't want to stay a little bit longer?

- I would mom but I left many things in the middle, I have to get back.

- Yes, I'm sure you have many things to do…now that you're not working!

His father:

- That's all right son, do as you will, you know you're always welcomed here.

His father hugs him:

- Have a nice journey.

His brother hugs him and looks at him with understanding:

- Have a nice trip.

As he enters the bus his mother says:

- When will you get a car?

- I'm better off without one, you know I don't need it…bye…

***

He enters the bus and finds a seat.

(Music: Know your past – Morgan Heritage)

The bus takes off. As he travels he remembers how, when he was a kid, when his parents went out, his grandmother, who was very religious, she was always reading to him from the Bible, at the bed before sleeping, the "adventures" of Jesus Christ.

(Music fades out)

After a stop of the bus, some people enter. A man in his fifties with grey hair and a beard, looking a bit wise, sits by his side.

John looks pondering and after a while this guy turns to him:

- You look very thoughtful, what is on your mind?

- I'm coming back from a funeral and I was thinking something from my early childhood.

- Funeral, ah… "Blessed is he who hath a soul, blessed also is he who hath none but woe and grief to the one who hath only it's seed".

John ponders a little and says:

- I didn't really get this…what do you mean that someone has a soul and…what was the rest?

- Was your grandmother a good person?

- Yes, I believe she was a really good person.

- Ok…but was she…*consciously* good?

He ponders a little and says:

- What do you mean when you say consiously good?…he stares in front of him and realizes:

- …and how did you know that it was my grandmother that died? and turns surprised to the stranger but the seat beside him is empty!

At this point he suddenly wakes up and looks beside him to see the man reading a book. They exchange a smile. He turns to the window with an amused face and stares outside.

***

He enters his appartment in the city. It has much stuff inside it, things hanging from the ceiling, on the wall, in an artistic but a bit chaotic style.

He finds his girlfriend packing some things of her in a suitcase.

He tells her, in a serious tone:

- So that's it! You're leaving me… just like that… when I'm away, without saying a word… I know… you would leave me a note…, he pretends to search, Where's the note? What have you written?

- I'm glad you never lose your sense of humour, how was it?

He kisses her:

- It was ok…family-like, how are you, is your apartment ready?

- Yes the painting has finished and now I have to rearrange my stuff, so… I have to leave now, you caught me almost at the door.

- Oh…I hoped you'd stay and talk a little…

- Why did something happen?

- Yes, a lot of things happened…in my mind, I have all these thoughts…about life and where we're going.

- Oh baby, I can't talk now… I know where I'm going… I'm going to my appartment to rearrange my stuff…we'll talk in the afternoon.

- In the afternoon I'm seeing the guys.

- Ok, tomorrow then.

- "Tomorrow is another day…"

- Of course it is another day and a very good one to talk…
Oh come on, I really have to go.

- All right…

On the door he kisses her goodbye:

- Ok, goodbye…see…I told you, you were leaving me.

She gives him a "serious" look.

He smiles:

- Come on, you know I'm joking.

- Are you? Maybe deep inside, you want me to leave you.

Now he gives her a "serious" look.

She smiles:

- Now, I'm joking…Bye.

- Bye.

***

He enters in a bar, he looks for his friends. His friends are,
Matthew the intellectual-type of man, Mark always

emotional and Luke the instictive-type, he never thinks a lot neither is very emotional about things.

John sees them and goes to them:

- Hey, everybody.

Matthew:

- Hey John, how did everything go?

- Everything went fine…

Mark:

- How are your folks?

- Good, good, everybody is ok.

Luke:

- Ok…so…let's drink to your freedom!

- Freedom?

Mark:

- You quit your job, didn't you?

- Oh, yes I did.

Luke:

- So let's drink to that!

They all drink.

Mark:

- You don't look very good, what's going on? …How are things with Kate?

- Things are ok…but…I don't know…

- Something is missing, right?

- Yeah… I feel very close to her but…I don't know…I can't imagine myself living the rest of my life with her…if I did, it would be like…

- Compromising!

- Yeah! Exactly! Compromising…it would be like depriving myself from the opportunity of a more complete relationship.

Matthew:

- That's what compromising is all about.

Luke:

- Yeah…preventing yourself from the unknown…

They all look at him.

Matthew:

- That was deep… and raises his glass, No to compromising!

All together 'No to compromising!' and they all drink.

John:

- I don't know, maybe this relationship is one of the things that are holding me back…maybe it's coming to an end…

Mark:

- Coming to an end…are you sure? This is serious…you've been with her for how long…three years…you better think it twice…I wouldn't end, if I were you, such a long relationship.

They all look at him.

Matthew:

- But you just said that his relationship is a compromise.

John:

- Yeah…and you just drunk to "No compromising".

Mark:

- I know what I said but on the other hand, if you brake up with her, are you sure that you'll find something better, at least with her you have something.

Matthew:

- Oh you are crazy, what you're saying is the definition of compromising, John says that this relationship is holding him back, he wants to move on.

John:

- Not necessarily move on to another relationship, I mean move on with my life…find something…

Matthew:

- Oh I didn't mean that…if you don't plan to search for another girlfriend, then you shouldn't brake up with Kate, at least not until you decide to search for another.

John:

- You're crazy too! Even more than him, if that's not compromising then what is?

Luke:

- John you're right, these guys don't have a clue what they're talking about, but even so, I think you're a little mixed up too, what's the problem, anyway, with Kate? Hasn't everything been great, up to now?

- Yeah everything has been great but I feel we're not made up exactly for each other, we have lots of common but we're not really cut for each other. Let me give you an example, we both love the sea, ok?

Mark:

- All right.

Luke:

- Ok.

Matthew:

- Go on…

John:

- So, when we get to the sea, I want to swim…

Luke:

- That's normal, what else can you do?

John:

- I also want to admire the sea…

Mark:

- Right…to see its beauty.

John:

- And I want to talk about the sea, to realize its existence.

Matthew:

- That's more meaningful…

John:

- But Kate is just the swimming-type, she wouldn't want to talk about the sea nor sit quietly and feel the sea…not that we don't talk or have feelings for each other but she's more the kind of type who always wants to do something… do you understand?'

Luke:

- Yes I do, she's how a woman must be.

Mark:

- I don't really understand…

Matthew:

- Neither do I, do you mean she doesn't like to conversate? That's the most important thing in a relationship.

Mark:

- I don't agree, the most important thing in a relationship is the feelings…

Luke:

- Both of you, you don't know what you're talking about, the most important thing in a relationship, is in general the physical contact and particularly, sex.

Matthew:

- Yes, I agree with that, sex is important.

Mark:

- I'm with you on that guys, and raises his glass 'Sex is important!

The others drink with him, except John, he just stares at them:

- Anyway guys, you're missing the point.

Luke:

- What point?

- The point is that Kate doesn't complete me in all the sides of myself.

They all nod their heads with understanding:

Matthew:

- If that's the situation, perhaps you should brake up with her…

Mark:

- I agree there is no future to a relationship like this…

Luke:

- No future…sex problems…no future…

John:

- Oh you're all nuts!!

They all drink.

***

Next morning.

He walks at his neighbourhood. He passes by a grocery store and waves the grocer:

- Good morning Mr. C.

- Good morning to you too, my dear youngman and may God make every day of your life be full of love and happiness as this day today is.

John, as he walks by, repeats, at the same time with him, the grocer's words, looking that he is very well acquainted with them:

- "Good morning to you too, my dear youngman and may God make every day of your life be full of love and happiness as this day today is".

A woman picks up some stuff from the grocery and not very pleasantly she says:

- Can you help me with these please?

- Of course, my dear lady, I'll be glad to be of some assistance to you.

***

He goes to a park. He sits on a bench and watches the people around him.

Matthew approaches. He sits on the bench with John:

- I knew I'd find you here.

- Yes, when I'm not working I always enjoy sitting here…

- How do you feel today?

- I'm trying to have a day full of love and happiness but I don't know if I can manage it…

- You've seen the grocer guy again? He still says his same old wishes?

- Yeah, he is a little bit strange…he says each time the same thing and more than that, he always looks like he won the lottery…

- I wouldn't worry about him, he is just a weird guy but I do worry about you… you looked very distant last night…what's bothering you? Is it Kate?

- No, it's not her…thanks for your concern, but there's no need to worry… I just have this feeling that there is something more in all that… and he points with a gesture to everything around him.

- Aren't you a bit old to question these things? We had this kind of thoughts when we were eighteen, why do you want something more than all this… and he points all around him too, isn't this enough? You have plenty of time in front of you to live a wonderful life; don't depress yourself with such thoughts.

- I'm not getting depressed but I need to know what life is all about and what's my place in it.

Matthew looks at his watch:

- As far as I'm concerned, for the time being, life wants me to be at my work, because if my boss doesn't find me in my place, I'll have to search with you a place in life.

John isn't smiling.

- I'm joking John…but I have to go.

- Yes I know, have a nice day.

- You too, and smiling, and I hope it will be full of love and happiness…

John smiles.

***

He is left alone. He looks around him and sees a lady looking at him, from the opposite bench at a small distance. She has an opened book in her legs.

He waves at her:

- Hi! How are you?

- Never better, while she is still looking at him.

Feeling a little awkward he says:

- I see you have a book right there, is it interesting?

- Oh yes, it is.

- What is it about?

- Now I was reading for the need to "pray unceasingly".

- Oh… and what exactly means to "pray unceasingly"?

- It means that we have to pray all the time for every little thing that concerns us.

- Yeah, it sounds good…but I don't think it's possible… or logical… how can we pray all the time? Or why should we have to pray all the time?

- Because if we don't "pray unceasingly" nothing is possible.

He ponders a little:

- ...Ok... do you mind if I come and sit over there... so we can have this conversation without having to "shout" to each other?

- Of course, I'd like you to come.

- So... you say that I'll have to pray if I want to get there?

- ...If you want to come, you have to pray.

- Ok, then I won't pray and we'll see what happens.

He gets up:

- I'm coming... and he starts walking, he looks at his right "nothing from right..." he looks at his left "nothing from left..." he looks up "nothing from..." and at the same time he walks with his foot up to a pile of dog dung and says "Oh... shit!"

The lady laughs:

- Yes indeed, that's what it is...

John walks disappointed back to his bench and looks for something to clean his shoe:

- ...That was just bad luck...

The lady continues laughing:

- I don't know what it was, I only know that you didn't manage to get here!

- Ok but when I clean my shoe, I can still come, I don't think there is a second pile of dung waiting for me to step on it.

She laughs:

- Oh, you can never know…

A small child comes running to her:

- Grandma, grandma, we have to go, mom's waiting for us in the car.

- All right, darling. Have a nice day my dear boy, it was very nice talking to you.

- For me too, not for my shoe, but for me it was.

She laughs.

John:

- You too have a nice day.

***

Later the same afternoon he is in front of a computer and searches in the internet. He types the word "prayer". The phone rings and he picks it up:

- Hello?

- Hey, John.

- Oh, hi Kate.

- I'm calling to cancel it for tonight, I can't come over.

- Oh really and I wanted to talk to you.

- About what? Is something wrong?

- Oh no, no, I just have all these thoughts in my mind and something really funny happened today…

- I'm sorry John but I haven't finished all these things I have to do…

- Couldn't they wait for one day and see each other today?

- If it's so important for you John, of course they can wait…

- Oh no, no, it's not that important…it doesn't matter, we'll talk tomorrow.

- Ok, thanks John, we'll talk tomorrow then, bye.

- Bye.

He looks a little bit dissapointed but then he cheers up again when he remembers his search in the internet.

***

(Music: Wake up and live – Bob Marley)

Next morning. He walks at his neighborhood; he passes by the grocery and waves the grocer:

(Music fades out)

- Good morning Mr. C.

- Good morning to you too, my dear youngman and may God make every day of your life be full of love and happiness as this day today is.

John, as he walks by, repeats the grocer's words:

- "Good morning to you too, my dear youngman and may God make every day of your life be full of love and happiness as this day today is".

Mr. C. shouts a little, so he can be heard from John who is walking away:

- I really mean these words I say to you each day and from day to day my wish for you is becoming stronger within me.

John, astonished, turns back:

- …Eh…Thank you Mr. C. I…

- I can tell looking from behind, by the way you shake your head, that you're saying something as you walk by…so it's easy to understand that you repeat my words…each and every time.

- Oh, I'm sorry, I didn't mean to offend you…

- I'm not offended at all, in fact it is rather amusing, you're a bit strange you know… you say every time something with no meaning at all for you and you never get bored!

- …!... You're right!… and all this time I thought you were the strange one!

- …I know, I know… Do you want to come inside so I can have a little company this beautiful day?

- Yes, of course, and upon entering, Mr. C. how come you've never asked my name?

- Oh I have a name for you.

- You have?

- Yeah! The parrot-boy!

They both laugh.

***

They go inside. They sit.

- I was wondering Mr. C., how come you always look so happy?

- I look happy because I am happy, God makes me happy.

- How God makes you happy and why doesn't he make all the other people, inluding me, happy?…And how can someone be happy, with all these bad things happening every day?

- You can't force someone to be happy; God doesn't want to force us to be happy. I used to be, when I was at your age, always miserable and ungrateful and at the same time so proud about myself… but when my "self", my false-self, led me to nowhere, then bad things, as you say, happened to me and I was able to see my empty pride and my empty self. So this "bad" that is all around us, maybe it has another purpose than the one we think, maybe it is not meant to torture us, maybe it is destined to wake us up. When bad things happened to me… that was when I woke up. Do you see dreams?

- Yes, I do.

- Do you see beautiful dreams?

- Yes, sometimes.

- When you see a nice dream, do you enjoy it?

- Yes, of course I do.

- When you see a beautiful dream do you want it quickly to end?

- No, I don't.

- What about when you see a bad dream, do you enjoy it?

- Of course not.

- Don't you want to wake up? Don't you usually wake up when it gets really bad?

- Yes, usually when the bad dream gets really ugly, then I wake up.

- It's the same with life; bad things always wake us up.

- Wake us up from what?

- From the sleep we take as life.

All this time a customer searches for vegetables. He isn't paying any attention to the conversation next to him. He says now:

- Do you have apples?

- No my dear sir, I'm sorry I haven't got any, it's not their season.

- Do you know where I can find some?

- Excuse me but perhaps you mean "when" you can find, dear sir?

- No I mean where.

- Oh I'm really sorry sir, I'm afraid I don't.

- Ok… he says and leaves annoyed.

- Have a nice day, my dear sir.

John:

- All this time I couldn't really understand what you were talking about but now I do… This man was really asleep, he didn't pay any attention at all to what we were saying, he had his mind only to the off-season fruits and I'm sure he doesn't look like someone who permits God to make him happy.

- That's true my boy.

- And only a shock of some kind would wake him up.

- That's also true but you must never be harsh with people…when someone wakes up he must never forget that he used to be asleep as well and he must always be sympathetic towards people who either aren't ready or they don't want to wake up.

Customers come inside.

John:

- I see you're getting busy so I have to leave but if you allow me I'd like to come again and talk with you.

- You're always welcomed.

On leaving:

- Mr. C.?

- Yes, my boy?

- How come, after all this time, you spoke to me today?

- You were seeing a nice dream all this time and I didn't want to wake you up, my dear parrot-boy…

They smile to each other with understanding.

- And now?

- Now you looked like not enjoying so much this dream of yours…

- … I think you're right… I don't know… thanks anyway Mr. C., have a nice day.

- You too my dear boy and may God make every day of your life be full of love and happiness as this day today is.

John listens to his wish on his way leaving without repeating and looking a little moved.

***

Later in the afternoon, he is at his appartment. Matthew arrives there. They sit.

Matthew:

- John, what's going on with you? You look awful.

- I'm depressed… I realized that my whole life has been meaningless up to this point.

- What are you talking about? Haven't you always been doing what you liked?

- Up to now I was leaving in a dream, I was just reacting to things… if something good happened I was happy, if something that I considered bad happened I was unhappy… I was gathering informations about everything around me, repeated them in a changed form and that I called thinking.

- You exaggerate, I've always thought of you as a smart guy.

- How can one be smart when he hasn't got a thought of his own!

- Oh come on now, you can't expect yourself to be a philosopher or something…

- I'm just talking about the ability of man to think… what is he, where is he heading to, what does he want… it's not thinking when you just respond to everything that happens around you with the best way you can find…just to get along with things…

- I can't really see what is your problem.

- The problem is me.

- Oh, I can see that…

- The problem is that there is no "me"… I feel empty inside, I don't know who am I, I don't know if I can even use the word "I". Who is "I" ?

- Oh that's serious, you have an identity crisis?

- I don't have control over my feelings, they are like wild horses that take control of me whenever they like, my thoughts are never original about anything, it's like I have some records playing in my mind that they respond to every situation…and what about that? he points to his body.

- What about what?

- My body! It's like I'm carrying a huge weight that I really don't know how I must handle it; it's like a huge responsibility that you have to deal with all of your life…feed it, clean it, protect it, exercise it…

- …..?!?…..

- Oh, I'm sorry… I don't want to trouble you with all that, it's just very strange, I feel like I don't exist, I feel that I have only the possibility to exist and that something must be done so this possibility can be actualized…

- …I think I get you in a way… myself sometimes I feel that I don't really know who am I and at these times it seems that I don't have any control over my life, everything just happens and I just go along with it and it's like my life is leading me nowhere… Mathew confesses and looks troubled.

- That's what I'm talking about! It seems that up to now my life has been moving on and I have been left somewhere behind, like I haven't done anything with it… I feel empty, my life is just passing me by…

Matthew "recovers":

- But I don't really see the point, why should you trouble yourself with these questions, I don't see why you should get distressed, everyone might feel like this from time to time but we always get over it… I have to say… I really worry about you…

The bell rings. All the friends and Kate are gathered.

***

John, his three friends and Kate are sitted in the living room. Everyone is talking cheerfully except John.

Kate:

- What's wrong John? Why are you like this?

- …Oh I'm sorry; I was just thinking something…

Matthew wants to cheer him up:

- You know guys… John made a confession to me, just before you came… he admitted that he is not as smart as he pretends to be all this time…

They all laugh.

Mark:

- So that's why you look so weird lately and off distance…you're trying to use your mind for once…

They all laugh.

Luke:

- Yeah, yeah you're right… he just said he was trying to think of something…

Mark to John:

- So… did you manage?

John:

- What?

Mark:

- To think!

They all laugh.

Matthew:

- Oh come on…spare him a second…that's not at all polite…look at him…he's so exhausted from trying to think!

They all laugh, John smiles…

Kate:

- So that was the thing you wanted to talk me about, to tell me that you're not smart… oh you don't have to worry… I already knew that and I've always liked you the way you are… and she hugs him.

They all laugh and John smiles politely.

Luke:

- John I want you to know that I'm with you, in this effort of yours.

They all laugh; John has a "frozen" smile at his face.

Mark:

- Yeah, that's for sure, even if your mind refuses to cooperate with you in all this thinking-effort, we'll be by your side.

They laugh.

Matthew:

- Yeah John we want you to know that we love you they way you are… you don't have to start using your mind…

They laugh.

Luke gets up laughing and goes to the kitchen, returns, sits and says:

- The beers are over…and I don't know if there's anything open at this hour…

Matthew:

- Don't worry… we'll think of something, and turns to John, Not you John…don't worry…

They laugh.

Mark:

- Yeah, you should take a rest, enough with this thinking effort…your head will explode!

They laugh.

John tries to look calm and smiling:

- I know a place where they must be open…I'll go and get some beers.

The others:

- All right, thanks John…

When John is at the door, Matthew says:

- Do you think he was offended?

Luke:

- No… John rarely gets offended…

Mark:

- Yeah, he was smiling…don't worry, he's ok.

They all look at each other and laugh a little.

***

(Music: Dream - Groundation)

John walks in the dark, he looks very sad and mizerable. After a while he passes by an open café and he sees inside Mr.C. sitting alone. He enters inside and goes to him.

(Music fades out)

- Hey Mr.C. …can I join you?

- Of course you can, my dear boy!

John sits. They look at each other.

Mr.C.:

- Come on tell me…

- …Oh I just don't know… I don't feel very much myself lately…

- That's good, that's good…

- How's that good?

- If you don't recognize all these things you were up to now as your "self", then you have a really big chance of finding your *true self*.

- …Yeah… I could never think of it like that… but it's true… and he starts cheering up.

- "You must sacrifice your false self with his deeds and be reborn to a new man."

John ponders over this. A small silence follows. John is getting down again.

Mr.C.:

- The resistance against your awakening is already bringing you down?

- …How could you know about that? …Yeah, it's like everyone around me suddenly stopped understanding me… and it's sadder because this lack of understanding comes from-

- The ones you love the most.

- Yes! How did you know that?

- It's always like this, it's sad but true but your beloved ones around you are as much asleep as everybody else and they will be the ones who will feel very awkward when they see that you're starting to be different…that you're trying to wake up.

- But if I talk to them, won't they listen to me? Shouldn't they listen?

- Even if you talked to them for a thousand years, they wouldn't listen to you, just because they can't listen to you…everyone has his own time…if you manage to wake yourself up and keep him awake, then some of your beloved ones might sense in a good way your change and they'll want this change for themselves and then they'll come and listen to you… You should never try to change someone, you should always try to change yourself… and the rest will follow.

- I don't know if I can do that… sometimes I'm really annoyed when I see that someone doesn't understand me.

- Try to remember what I told you about waking up. If a man wakes up from this sleep we call life, he shouldn't start being intolerant to other people who are still asleep because then he'll find himself, very quickly and without realizing it, in a worst position than before. This will happen because his attitude will throw him back to sleep, but this time it will be more difficult for him to wake up because he'll think himself as wide awake! Imagine how unpleasant would that be… to be as asleep as everybody else is but to believe that you're better than everyone else because you're the only one awake!

John ponders over all these. Silence.

John:

- I'm wondering how come you have all this knowledge about…

- The inner life of man?

- Yes, exactly…our inner world!

- "Seek and ye shall find."

- Yes but where should someone search? Nobody in our times wants to have anything to do with all these…

- When your thirst for discovering the truths that concern your inner world becomes irresistible, then you're becoming like some sort of magnet to everything than can help you towards this aim of yours.

- …I can understand that, if you're not interested in something then you are some sort of deaf and blind to it and if you have a sincere interest about a certain thing then it's like everything that has got to do with it, starts appearing in front of you…

 Mr. C. nods in aggreement.

- Mr. C there is another issue that is confusing me… You see, there are so many religions… and everyone thinks he is right. My grandmother admired Jesus Christ and was always talking me about him… I also like what the

Buddhists say about having sympathy towards all creatures… I'm confused with all this religion thing…

- All true religions have one and the same foundation… God and man finding himself… you're not a Christian or a Buddhist or a Muslim or a Jew just because you call yourself with that name. You're a true follower of a religion if you live according to its inner principles which for all the religions are the same: find yourself and God. If you do that, then on the outside you can be a Jew or a Hindu or even nothing at all, but inside, in your heart, you are both Buddhist, Muslim, Jew, Christian, Hindu and whatever else…
John ponders over all these.

John:

- Mr. C. can I come tomorrow morning by your shop so we can talk a little more? I won't stay long and bother you with your customers and your work.

- Of course you can come, you don't bother me, what I understand as God's will never bothers me… if God wants you to come, you'll come…

- All right then, I hope I'll see you tomorrow, goodnight.

- Goodnight, my dear boy.

***

He enters in his apartment in a cheerful mood. He sits with his friends and Kate in a very good mood. They all give him strange looks.

John:

- What?

Luke:

- What took you so long? Didn't you find any beers?

- Oh! I completely forgot about it! …probably my mind was too tired to remind me that.

Matthew:

- Tired from what?

- From all this thinking-effort I did earlier on… he says in a cheerful mood and waits the others to be amused.

Nobody laughs.

Mark:

- John, you're incredible… you're gone all this time and you come back empty-handed and you didn't even think of searching for beers!

- …I'm really sorry… I totally forgot about it… he apologizes and starts losing his good mood.

Silence.

John:

- Doesn't anybody want to know where I've been all this time?

Mark says at the same time:

- Sorry guys it's late for me and I've got to get up early tomorrow, I' ll listen to your story tomorrow John… Good night everybody, and upon leaving, Matthew you want to come?

Matthew:

- Yeah, I'm coming with you then, you can drop me by… you can tell us another time John, goodnight guys.

Silence.

Luke:

- I guess you two want to be left alone, so… I'm going too.

John has lost his good mood:

- …Yeah… ok… goodnight, anyway my story wasn't that interesting…

Kate:

- Oh, if that's so, then perhaps I could leave with Luke, if he can give me a ride home. I can't really spend the night here… I have to get up early tomorrow too… you don't mind, do you John?

- No, no I don't mind at all… ok, goodnight… thanks for coming…

She kisses him goodbye. He is left alone with no good mood at all.

***

Next morning. He arrives at the grocery shop, not in a good mood. He waves Mr.C. with a nod.

Mr. C. smiles to him with understanding and welcomes him inside. They sit.

John:

- I don't know if the problem is with me or with everybody else. It seems like I live in a world and all the rest live in a different one…

- Family, friends and the *right* girlfriend, are very important in life. But in order for a man to honor his family as they ought to be honored, he must first learn how to honor God seing Him as his spiritual family and in order to be faithful to his friends as he ought to be, he must be faithful to God seeing Him as his olny friend and in order to love his other half as it should be loved, he must first know how to love God as God loves him.

- …I don't feel as close to God as I should probably feel…

- That's very reasonable, in time you will… as long as you're on the right path of finding yourself, you'll discover that you're coming closer to God.

Silence.

John:

- Why did you emphasize the word "right" differently when you said "right girlfriend", if I observed correctly?

- Yes indeed, you observed correclty. Take yourself for example, do you have a girlfriend?

- Yes I do.

- You think she is the right *one* for you?

- Oh… I don't really know, I am a bit confused in this matter…but then again, I'm generally confused these days.

- I don't want to imply anything but when someone is confused, then his choices are confused as well… It's a fact that if your girlfriend is the right One for you, your other half as I prefer saying it, then she will support, even without realizing it, in this search of yours for your real self and that's because your real self is her real self too, if she is your other half.

- …I think I understand what you're saying… but what I'm certain of, is that she doesn't really, realizing it or not, support me lately… at least in the way I'd liked her to…

- You must be patient, when you will know your self, everything around you, will be different; some people might lose the importance that they have now for you in your life and some others might have more significance for you than they have now, or even new people might come into your life. You can never know what your change will bring; you can only know that is going to be for the best.

- How can I be sure of that? That I'm not going to make wrong choices, mistakes?

- Oh, there will be wrong choices and mistakes but this time you'll start learning from them. If you find your true self, you'll find God and believe me, everything gets better when you let God come into your life…

- …For the time being, I'm very glad that you have come into my life.

- Oh, I didn't tell you…I'm leaving tomorrow.

- Oh, really? On holidays or something? When you're getting back?

- I'm not getting back, I'm moving.

- Moving?… To where?…

- I'm moving to Australia.

John laughs:

- …Come on now…you're joking, right?

Mr. C, smiling, waves his head saying "no".

John:

- Oh… I can't believe what is happening… the only person I could talk with… And all this time you were next to me… why couldn't we have talked earlier?

- That wasn't possible, you weren't disappointed enough…

- Disappointed from what?

- From the dream we call life…

- Which now turns out to be a nightmare… what am I going to do without you?

- Perhaps it's better for you that I'm leaving. If I was to stay then perhaps you would get "hypnotized" by me, believing anything I tell you, without trying to verify for yourself the things I tell you. You could become satisfied with just listening…and that would mean…back to sleep again. Perhaps the fact that I'm leaving is one of the "bad things" that keep us awake…

- I don't know, perhaps you're right… but you should've told me this earlier…

- What would be the difference?

- …I don't know…I would be getting used to the idea that from now on I'll be on my own.

- Oh, but you're not on your own… you are with the One who is with each and every one of us… you are with God, and he points with his finger to his left.

John looks at his left wondering:

- Why are you pointing there?

Mr. C. laughs:

- I always like to do that… isn't it funny how people always point upwards when they refer to God… as if God sits on the sky above us in a far away distance…

- …yeah, but don't they always say that paradise is on heaven above, at the sky…

Mr. C. laughs more:

- Oh…, so, you too, believe that God sits above us and likes to watch your funny head moving towards all directions!

They both laugh.

Mr. C.:

- Earth is in space, what's down for the people at north, is up for the people at south… God is all around us, God is everywhere and God is also inside us… "Behold, the kingdom of God is within you" …that's why we're never alone… if we find God inside us.

John thinks over these words and says:

- I'm surely going to miss you…

- I'll miss you too.

- I'm really grateful for all these things you told me… goodbye and thank you very much, I wish the best for you!

- Goodbye my dear boy.

***

In the bar. Matthew, Mark and Luke are talking.

Mark:

- So what was this important thing you wanted to talk us about?

Matthew:

- The reason I wanted to see you is John…

Luke with understanding:

- Oh…yeah…

Mark nods with understanding too.

Matthew:

- I'm really concerned about him.

Luke:

- Yeah, he is acting very strange lately…

Mark:

- Yes, you're right, John always knew what he wanted and now…

Matthew:

- He is lost!

Mark:

- Though in a way, he looks more…

Luke:

- Serious.

Mark:

- Yeah…serious…

Matthew:

- Now that you say so, I think too, that he looks like he's getting to something new…something important…

Mark:

- And perhaps he's trying to tell us something and we just don't want to listen to him…

Matthew:

- Or on the other hand, he's asking for our help, to get himslef out of this sort of… deppresion, he's got himself into…

Luke:

- Yeah… it's difficult to tell what is really happcning…

Matthew:

- That's why I was thinking of seeing him, all of us, and talk with him, see what's on his mind perhaps we don't really pay attention to him all this time…

Mark:

- Yeah, you're right…we'll meet him tonight!

Luke:

- Yeah, I'll call him and arrange it.

Matthew:

- Ok! Tonight then!

Mark:

- Yeah! Tonight!

Luke:

- Tonight!

They're about to leave like they're on a mission but then they slow down and return to finish their drinks. They drink a little.

Matthew:

- So… what else?

They look a little "down".

But then Mark cheers up:

- Oh! …You won't believe who I saw today!

They start talking again and look again cheered up.

***

John is lying relaxed on his couch at his appartment looking thoughtful. The phone rings. He looks at it. It keeps ringing. He makes a small movement to get up and pick it up but decides not to answer and lies back again looking calmer and more relaxed. He returns to his thoughts but at the same time the doorbell rings. He looks surprised. The door bell rings and the phone keeps ringing.

He gets up and opens the door. He looks at Mark questioningly.

Mark:

- Hey John, I found the front entrance opened, how are you?

- I'm pretty fine thank you, how are you?... and he goes to the phone.

As he picks it up the front entrance's bell rings.

Mark says:

- Don't worry, I'll get that… Matthew is that you? Ok…

John looks a little upset as he answers the phone:

- Oh hey Luke, you forgot to tell me what?… You're coming tonight?… Ok, you've already arrived …oh, nothing… you'll be here in no time? …ok, see you.

They're all sitted. They all feel a little awkward except Luke.

John:

- I sense there is a certain…purpose in your visit?

Luke:

- Oh, no… we've just dropped by to see you. Why? …There must be a reason to visit you?

Matthew:

- That's true, we don't need a special reason to visit you…
but in fact we were saying that it would be good to get
together and talk… like we used to do…

Luke:

- Oh, yeah… we did say that…

Mark:

- Yes, we were saying that we don't talk very much lately
and you seem to have many things on your mind… so
perhaps you might want to talk about them…

John:

- If that's so… you did very well coming tonight… it's true,
we don't talk much lately and I really wanted to talk with
you guys… so, you did well… I'm glad you came…

Luke:

- Does anybody want to drink a beer? John do you have
any beers?

- Yes I do but I don't want to drink, I decided that I want
to abstain from alcohol for a while but if you want to drink
I can bring you some…

Mark:

- Why you don't drink anymore?

- Oh, I just want to keep my head clear, so I can be concentrated to these things that have been on my mind lately.

- Oh, that's good, if that's the reason then I'll keep my head clear, too! No beer-drinking for me tonight'.

Matthew:

- I'm with you guys, clear thought for tonight!

Luke:

- Personally, beer helps me think more clearly! …Anyway, I don't want to drink alone… so, no beer tonight! …you know we should drink to that…

Mark:

- To what?

Luke:

- To "no beer drinking tonight!"

They all look at him.

Matthew:

- I think he means it!

Mark:

- He's nuts, of course he means it!

They all laugh except Luke.

Matthew:

- But I must say, I'm a little hungry…I don't think if we eat something it will be harmful to us!

John:

- No, I don't think so… you want me to go and prepare something for all of us…

Mark:

- I'd like that if it's not so much trouble.

John:

- No, not at all. Luke you want me to count you in?

Luke:

- If everybody is eating, I'm eating too, yeah count me in.

John goes to the kitchen looking cheered up.

Mark:

- I think it was good we came.

Matthew:

- Yeah, everything's going fine, I think it's good for John.

Mark:

- Perhaps we jumped into conclusions…

Matthew:

- Yes, he looks like he's getting back to his old self again.

Luke goes and opens the television.

Matthew:

- Hey, what are you doing? Close the TV!

Mark:

- Yeah, we came to see John, not watch TV, close it down.

Luke:

- Oh yeah I know, I just want to see the score, it's a very important game of the season.

In the kitchen, John makes some sandwiches and shouts to them:

- It won't take too long guys…I'm coming…

The others shout back:

- Take your time John, don't worry…

When everything is almost done, Mark enters in the kitchen, opens the fridge and gets some beers:

- Do you want any help, John?

- No, everything is almost done…I thought you weren't going to drink any beers tonight…

Mark:

- Oh, come on, what's wrong with drinking one beer, and upon leaving, you worry too much John.

John starts bringing the dishes. He finds all of them in front of the TV, really absorbed. They don't even notice John and the food he's bringing. He leaves some dishes on the table in front of them and goes to get everything else. On the last things Matthew still absorbed says:

- Oh thanks John, you need any help?

John has lost his entire good mood and says:

- No, no, I'm fine…

He sits and eats a little, watching TV without realy seeing. The others are really enjoying the game.

John leaves his food and gets up. He goes to the door and opens it and upon closing it, Luke says:

- Hey John, where are you going?

John:

- Don't worry, I'll be back…

Luke:

- Ok… if you can, bring some more beers, will you?

- I'll try to remember it…, he says and leaves.

***

(Music: Who the Cap Fit – Bob Marley)

He looks sad. He is going for a walk. He finds a phone and calls Kate. The phone rings and the answering machine answers:

- Hi, I'm Kate, I'm not here right now but if you really want to talk to me, you should call back later.

He hangs up the phone very disappointed. He goes for a walk and passes by the café where he had sat with Mr. C. and gets even more disappointed. He sits on a bench and looks around without really seeing, whilst it seems like the disappointment will be imprinted permanently on his face.

(Music fades out)

***

He returns home late having the same face expression. Everybody has left. He cleans up a little still with the same face expression.

***

Next morning he goes for a walk having the same face expression. He passes by the closed grocery store and the dissapointment in his face looks like is getting uglier. He goes to the park, he sits on his bench and looks to the opposite bench where he had seen the lady but there's nobody. His face is becoming uglier. An old man approaches and sits at the opposite bench. The old man looks at John. John with an unchanged face expression looks back at him as someone on whom all his hopes are laid on.

The old man says:

- Hey, young man, what's bothering you? You don't look very well.

John replies:

- I feel like I'm all alone in this world.

- Aren't we all alone? We are born alone and we die alone.

- But someone told me, that we're never alone, God is always with us.

- Oh, I have stopped believing in all these fictions long time ago. Do not kid yourself son, we are all alone in this world and the only thing we can do is get used to that.

John gets up:

- Why am I wasting my time, you just wouldn't understand, you're just as asleep as everybody else is! he says to himself and leaves with an angry face expression. His dissapointment has turned to anger.

***

(Music: Judge Not – Morgan Heritage)

He starts walking and looking at things in a judgemental way. First he sees a woman yelling at her child and the child crying. He moves on to leave the park and sees two women sitting on a bench disagreing in a harsh way and a few steps away their children are starting to fight each other. He gets to the street and sees all the cars with their noise and pollution; he waits to cross the street because there are lots of cars and realizes the unecessairy movement of all these people with all possible means towards all directions. He manages to cross the road and continues walking, seeing things.

He sees an overweight man eating and on the side of the road a thin beggar; he sees an elderly man looking wealthy and a pretty young woman at his side; he sees someone throwing garbages down and very near a small child uncovering a gift and throwing the covering down; he looks at the faces of the people around him and they all look like they're lost in their thoughts, most of them with unhappy faces not seeming to realize anything that goes on around them. They all walk in a hurry, towards all directions.

He sees people around him talking to their cell-phones and then he sees two young boys smoking and one of them anwsering to his cell-phone; he sees walls with ugly graffiti; he sees two young boys in extreme punk appearances; he goes on and sees people on drugs; people sleeping at the side of the road with empty bottles by their sides; he sees a very expensive car with his driver looking very proud of it.

He sees the stores full of unecessairy products attracting the eyes of the customers. He sees a window of a shop with some fancy useless expensive decorative stuff and very near to it another window which is exactly the same only it has useless stuff of another kind, it has "feng-shui" things, small statues of gods and godesses and other similar stuff; he looks at the name of the store, it's called "Spiritual Awakening".

He goes on and sees "hidden" video-stores with pornographic material; he sees someone yelling at his girlfriend; some pollicemen arresting a guy; he sees a biological-health-food store which is empty and near by a hod-dog stand point and a line waiting to buy.

Now he walks fast making rounds around himself to see all the people looking totally indifferent one towards the other, with unhappy faces, "day-dreaming" as they walk. He himself looks very unhappy and he starts walking with his head lowered down.

(Music fades out)

He approaches a man climbed on a box who is shouting continually "Jugde not less you be judged" "Judge not less you be judged".

John passes him by without pay attention to him, but suddenly, as the man is just behind him, he listens very clearly to "Judge not less you be judged".

He turns surprised to the man who shouts and the man climbed to the box, immediately turns to John shouting in a very loud voice:

- YOOOU! YOU ARE A DEMON! YOU WILL BUUURN ETERNALLY IN HEEELL! YOU! YOU DESERVE ETERNAL PUNISHMENT!

John from the unexpected "attack" falls down on his back completely surprised by the loud voice of the man and as waking up from a dream starts laughing.

The man:

- LAAAUGH! LAUGH ALL YOU LIKE! YOUR ETERNAL MIZERY APPROACHES! YOU SHALL BE CONDEMNED TO THE DEEEPTHS OF HELL! BUUURN IN HELL!

John tries to say, laughing at the same time:

- I'm really sorry, I'm not laughing at you, I'm laughing at myself.

And at this moment someone picks him up, helps him to stand up. John doesn't realize this immediately but when he gets up he sees a man who looks like a "criminal":

- You ok man?

- Yeah, yeah… I'm ok, and before he has the time to thank him, the guy leaves.

The climbed man has now lost his interest in John.

John smiles and leaves.

***

He is now at his apartment, looking excited. He searches on the internet everything that has to do with religions, Christianity, Judaism, Hinduism, Buddhists, Muslims; he prints and reads and ponders. He has also a Bible in which he notes some passages. He is in a constant vigilance as he searches, reads and ponders. He doesn't look like concluding to anything, though he seems satisfied with what he's doing.

At some point he stops:

- Now I really think that my head will explode, I need some fresh air.

He leaves his appartment and goes for a walk. He walks relaxed not really paying attention to anything when he suddenly notices a church. He looks surprised and says to himself:

- How come I haven't thought this earlier? Maybe here I'll find the answers…

He enters. He looks around and sits on a sit in the front row. A priest notices him.

John waves with a polite nodding. The priest approaches.

The priest:

- Hello, my child.

- Hello, father.

- Do you want to talk about something? Is there anything troubling you?

- Yes father… you see, I don't know how else to put it but I feel empty inside me…

- Don't say that my child, you're not empty.

- I can't seem to find true meaning in anything, everything seems vain…

- Have you read the Bible my child, only there you can find true meaning, only in Jesus Christ.

- I have read it but I don't think I truly understand it.

- You must read it many times, my child.

- No, I don't think that will help, I feel that there is something hidden in it, that I can't get to find… I don't know, perhaps I'm not ready yet…

- There's nothing hidden, my child, you just have to read it many times with faith, without questioning it and you'll understand it.

- That's the problem, I can't stop questioning it… I can't take most of things literally… it's absurd. For example, I can't believe that there is such thing as an eternal damnation of man in hell…

- My child, this is what Jesus Christ taught; you have to believe in it.

- I don't know… I'm not sure what Jesus Christ truly taught, I'm sensing that there is something more in all that…

- My child, you shouldn't trouble yourself like this, you will only confuse your mind.

- Tell me father, what is the soul? And what about the religions that believe in reincarnation, how can I be sure that I won't live again another life? …There are millions of people believing that…

- No my child, reincarnation is a lie, you should guard yourself from these kind of lies, they will only mislead you. Believe only in what Jesus Christ taught.

- But father, what if we don't really have a soul? But only the potential of building a soul? What if when Jesus Christ said that we have to save our souls, talked about actualizing the potential we have for a soul?…

- My child, I can see that you are already misled. What kind of talking is this? Of course we have a soul. How is possible not having a soul?…

- Why then was Jesus talking about a second birth? …I know I have a body, I sense it and I can talk about it. I also know that I have feelings and thoughts, both of them are very real to me, too. But what about my soul? Why I don't know anything about it? Are my feelings and my thoughts my soul? These are changing all the time… one day I'm feeling happy, next day I don't… I have all these different kinds of thoughts, all these contradictory and confusing thoughts… are these my eternal soul? How can this be?

- You're talking very strange my child, I'm afraid I can't be of any help to you, perhaps you should seek… professional help?

John gets up looking cheerful:

- No father, you've been of great help to me, I finally think I'm getting somewhere… Thank you for listening me, no one really does these days…Thank you, goodbye.

As he leaves, the priest tells him:

- Pray God to guide you.

- I will father, I will… Thank you, goodbye.

***

Next day. He wakes up cheerfully. He gets ready to go somewhere and listens to his messages on his answering machine.

- Hey John, it's Matthew… you know, we're very dissapointed of you, you left us again at your house waiting for you… you never call or answer our calls… what's happening to you? Instead of improving yourself, you're turning to someone very unpleasant… anyway… call me…

Kate:

- John… where have you been lost? …you know, I feel neglected, you act very indifferently towards me and lately it seems like you're only concerned with yourself… what's going on with you? Call me.

His mother:

- John, hey… you haven't called at all, how are you? I'm a little concerned about you… You're not working now, don't tell me you don't have enough time to make a phone call… your father also wants to talk with you… try to think a little bit of your parents too… we love you, bye.

John starts loosing his cheerfulness:

- It's a conspiracy! …I can't believe that, whenever I try to pick myself up…it's a conspiracy!

He goes outside. As he walks down the street someone yells at him from a car:

- Hey you!

John turns to him.

And the other man with no reason at all, yells at him:

- Fuck off! and gives him the finger.

John is amazed and a small grief takes over his face.

He goes on walking trying to realize what happened when someone who runs, knocks him down and goes on running.

John gets up when a policeman runs by his side chasing the guy and at the same time, two other policemen who came

running too and are obviously too tired to go on, "attack"
on John:

- Why didn't you stop him?

John:

- I didn't even see him coming.

The policemen:

- What do you mean you didn't see him coming?

- Perhaps you're working together?

- Yeah, who was he? Your partner?

- What is his name?

- Did he give you anything?

- Yeah, we saw you pretending to fall.

- Search him!

- Get him on the wall!

They put him on the wall and spread his legs to search him.

John tries to defend himself but they don't let him speak.

Two old women pass by:

- Ch,ch,ch… the youth of today…always up to
something…

- What a shame!

The policemen don't find anything illegal on him and let him go:

- Next time you should be more careful.

- Yeah, you should try to help our work and not standing in our way.

- You're lucky we don't bust you in.

The policemen leave and some people give him strange looks.

John goes on having lost his good mood and at the same time he looks surprised with all these things happening to him. He then sees a bookstore where it seems he was getting at and which is selling books on psychology and spirituality.

He enters. He looks around and tries to appear, despite what happened to him, as more polite as possible. An employee approaches him:

- How can I help you sir?

- Oh, I just want to have a look, I'll tell you if I need any help.

- I'm sorry sir but you can't fool around here, I would appreciate it if you could tell me what are you searching for.

John is amazed by this attitude but tries to remain polite:

- If that's so… I would like to find books concerning man's soul…

- You're not helping me that much, could you be a little more specific sir? We have plenty of books on this subject.

- Oh, I don't know, I would like to read something about the soul of man but I don't really know what exactly. Couldn't you recommend me something?

- I'm not a book critic, sir. Have a look here and there…, and shows him a huge place with books, but please do not touch anything, if you want to buy something, I'll give it to you.

- Oh… ok, you've been of a great help…

He starts looking and mechanically approaches a book with his hand, to have a look at it.

The employee:

- I think I told you not to touch anything.

John gets irritated:

- But how on earth will I know what I want to buy?

- Please do not raise your voice sir, we're a serious bookstore here.

John says in a low voice:

- Yes I can see that…, and then, ok, thank you and goodbye.

He leaves and now sadness covers his face as he walks back to his appartment. As he walks, he passes by a dog which is chained at a column and starts barking at him. The dog gets him scared but he turns to it:

- Nice dog, nice dog.

The dog keeps barking and at the same time someone shouts:

- Hey, don't mess with the dog. Get away from there you freak.

He is really amazed and sad but not angry and moves on.

***

(Music: Live it up – Groundation)

He is at his appartment at his couch, completely devastated, hugging himself, looking thoughtful. But then he remembers the employee's behaviour at the bookstore and gets amused. He starts thinking over all the "bad things" that happened to him and his reactions to them: his friends making jokes about him and himself with a "frozen" smile; his friends watching TV and himself leaving; the guy who called him a demon; the messages on the answering macine and his reaction to them; the guy who "gave" him the finger; the policemen; the dog; and then he starts assuming an erect posture, looking truly happy and grateful for all his "lessons". He opens his arms in the air, like wanting to hug all over the world and looks now, remembering all these things, as if he has love for all and everything.

***

(Music fades out)

At a park. He sits on the grass looking truly happy.

Mark arrives there, sees him and approaches him:

- Hey John.

- Hey.

They sit together without talking. John looks happy but Mark is not in a good mood.

Matthew arrives in the same way and sits with them:

- Hey.

- Hey.

John smiles, Mark doesn't, neither Matthew.

Luke arrives too and sits with them:

- Hey.

- Hey.

- How come we're meeting here? We've never been here before.

John:

- I wanted to meet you in a new place, because I feel like a new man.

The others nod "ok" without any enthousiasm.

John:

- Now we're all together, first of all, I wanted to tell you that I'm really sorry for my attitude all this time but I was really confused with where my life was heading to. I must admitt that I've reached to the point of questioning whether you were true friends of mine or not, but now I know that I'm grateful for you being my friends and I'm really sorry for having doubts.

His friends start overcoming their bad mood.

Luke:

- Oh come on John, that's ok, we all have our bad times.

Mark:

- Yeah, you don't need to apologize, we know you love us.

Matthew:

- Yes, John, don't worry about us… the only problem was that we've been worrying about you.

John:

- I knew you would understand. The main reason though, I wanted to see you, is that I knew you worried about me and I wanted to tell you that you don't need to worry anymore. There are a lot of things I realized all this time and there are a lot more that I still have to find out, but I discovered one thing that I know now beyond any doubt. Up to now, my life was leading me to nowhere, time was just passing by… but now I found the way to live every day of my life as wholly as possible… and this way is through love. Everyday I will try to love *consciously* everything that exists... Now I know who I want to be… the one God wants me to be, I want to be love, my true self must be built on love… Now I have a reason to live. I want to build my soul, to build it on love. On *conscious love* about everything that exists. In the same way that I eat everyday to build and maintain my body, in the same way that I perceive everyday all the things happening around and inside me feeding thus my thoughts and feelings, in the same way I must be filled everyday with love so I can build my soul, my true self, me!

His friends are speechless and moved.

Silence.

Mark hugs him:

- I wish for you to find all the strenth you need for that.

John is truly happy, the others look thoughtful and faint smiles of happiness start appearing on their faces.

***

Next day John goes to his park. He goes and sits to his bench. He sees at the opposite bench the lady he had once met. They look each other with understanding.

John:

- I prayed I could see you once more, if it was God's will.

She nods with understanding.

John:

- Can I come over there to ask you something that is on my mind?

The lady smiles:

- I don't know, can you?

- If I pray for it… I think I can.

He gets up and goes to her bench.

She claps her hands with joy:

- You did it, good for you… now, what is this thing you wanted to ask me about?

- It might sound silly but I'm really wondering, can really prayer bring someone closer to God?

She looks thoughtful and then she says:

- Prayer among other things is a form of remembrance…

- Remembrance of what?

- Remembrance of yourself…

- I don't really understand that, what do you mean when you say "remembrance of myself"?

- People constantly forget themselves; there are so many things both outside and inside them that distract their attention from themselves. People get identified with everything around them… they wake up in the morning and perhaps they will realize a little bit themselves but then the whole day passes by and the night comes and they get back to sleep, and then they might remember again that they were they themselves that went through all these things in that day. Sometimes people forget themselves for whole weeks or even for months or even worst for years.

- I think I understand… let me give you an example to see if I got this right… It's like when we watch a movie or when we read a book and we are really absorbed in it… it's like we don't exist… and then someone or something interrupts us and it's like we wake up, we realize that we have completely forgot ourselves, that we have become the movie we're watching or the book we're reading… so at that moment we'll remember ourselves for a minute… but then we'll go on watching the movie or reading the book and we might again remember ourselves when the movie or the book finishes…

- I think you got this right.

- And what does prayer has to do with all this?

- If you can manage to remember to pray within you, if you can remember to pray whenever you want, then you can remember yourself and be… yourself.

John looks like enlightened:

- Oh… now everything is getting clear… yeah… if for example something bad happens and instead of getting identified with it and respond towards it with my old ways, I can remember pray, then I can also remember to respond towards it with any way I want… or when I feel negativity about something, if I don't identify with it and manage to remember praying, I'll be able to remember myself and control this negative emotion of mine…

- And everyone must have his own prayer, everyone must be himself…

- Oh, I know what my prayer should be… "God give me the strength to love consciously, each and every day, all that exists".

She nods with understanding:

- If you remember to pray, you can remember yourself…

- So you can also remember God…

She nods.

John:

- So, prayer does bring you closer to God…and yourself…

- But you have to pray… what word you used…consciously! …yes, you have to pray consciously or else-

- You pray as a parrot!

She laughs and nods "yes".

John:

- You know, someone used to call me parrot-boy!

She laughs more:

- Really? …Yes, now that I watch you more carefully, you remind me of a parrot I used to know…

They laugh.

John:

- You used to know a parrot?!

- Oh, yes I did…and it was exactly like you!

They both laugh.

Kate suddenly appears, looking a bit sad:

- Hey John.

He is not very surprised:

- Oh, hey Kate.

- Hello madam, I'm sorry for interrupting…

The lady:

- Oh no, not at all, we had finished our little chat, hadn't we my dear boy?

John:

- Oh yes we did.

The lady:

- So, I have to get going…nice to meet you miss, and to John, I really enjoyed our chat.

- Me too, I'm grateful for your help.

She laughs:

- Oh come on now, goodbye.

- Goodbye.

***

Kate:

- I'm sorry John I interrupted you but I couldn't find you home and I wanted to see you… Who was her? A new friend of yours?

- Yes, you could say that. I wanted to see you too…

- Yeah… we haven't been seeing each other lately… I feel somewhat left behind… you have new friends… you can never be found… but it's ok, now we're together…

- That's why I wanted to see you Kate… a lot of new things happened to me… and I realized a lot about myself and us…

- I'm glad for you but what did you realize about us?

- I realized that we're not, as they say, each other's half, we're not made for each other…

- After all this time, you say now we're not made for each other? …And what about what we feel for each other… you don't have any feelings for me anymore?

- Kate, the main thing I feel for you is love but-

- Oh, you shouldn't talk about love… since you want us to brake up, you shouldn't talk about love… I, love you but …, she stops… and suddenly "explodes", Anyway, that's so typical of you John, never caring for other people's feelings. You have always your jokes and your good mood but in fact all these are fake… you just hide behind them your incompetence to have any true feelings about anything except for yourself.

John is about to say something but he looks like he's remembering something and stops. He only looks at her with affection and remains calm.

Kate:

- Good old-John, cares only for himself…, and she gets up to go.

As she leaves, she turns back to him:

- And you want to know something else- but she stops and looks at him, remaining truly calm, looking at her with love.

She sits again with him:

- Oh, I'm really sorry John, I don't know what has got into me… you know I don't believe any of these things I said… I wouldn't tell you such things not even for a joke …

He hugs her:

- Don't worry Kate, I know…

- Oh, John I really love you…

- Kate, it's true, what I feel for you is love but I know we're not meant to spend our lives together.

She laughs a little:

- To be honest, I was always a little scared of this thought… so I always tried not to think about it…, and she laughs more.

John:

- I know there is someone for you to complete you in a way I could never do… and I know there is someone for me too.

- …Yes we've always been so different…

- That's what I'm trying to say, we were alike only in a very small part of ourselves…

Kate ponders a little:

- I'm starting now to wonder how could we be together all this time…, and she laughs, but still, I have feelings for you and I will feel very lonely…

- You don't have to change your feelings towards me but in time you will see me as a friend… I really feel love for you; we don't have to lose our mutual appreciation.

- Yes, that's what I feel for you… appreciation and respect, thank you for everything…

- I thank you too… Yes, now we can move on to something we've never had… to a friendship.

- Yes, true friendship based on mutual appreciation and love… don't forget me John, whatever you do in your life…

- You know I won't…

They hug each other.

Kate gets up:

- I've got to go now John… I have to realize what happened, thank you for being the way you are… you've changed… I don't know in what way exactly… but you look changed… you look more…You… anyway… we'll talk, ok?

- Of course, whenever you want me I'll be there, wherever I might be…

On leaving:

- Why… you're planning to go a journey or something?

- I think so, yes… but you'll hear from me…

- Ok, bye John.

- Bye Kate and may God make every day of your life be full of love and happiness as this day today is.

Kate looks at him questioningly and waves at him. John is left alone and looks truly happy.

***

He enters in the bookshop he had visited, takes a look around and instead of seeing the employee he is looking for, he sees a beautiful woman. He is astonished. The woman turns towards him and when she sees him, she looks astonished, too. They have a moment of mutual recognition.

John:

- Hey…

- Hey… … …How can I help you?

- …I wanted to see an employee of yours, he tells her and describes him.

- Yes, I know who you mean, he's not working today…

- Oh, I would really appreciate it if you could thank him on my behalf… he doesn't really know me but he was of great help to me… just tell him that a satisfied customer thanked him…

- Oh, ok I will… excuse me for saying that… but it is a little strange… usually people want to complain about this specific employee… and you… you want to thank him!

- Oh, yes, he truly helped me… not in the ordinary way though but he was of some important assistance to me…

- Ok then, I'll give him your message, I'm glad… I think it will be good for him… he surely needs some support of this kind…

- Ok, so now I thank you too, for being so kind and helpful.

- Oh, I'll be glad to do that… but why don't you come back another day and tell him yourself…

- I'd like to but I have many things to do, I'm leaving this city…

- Really? That's a coincidence… I'll be leaving in a few days too. I got tired of the city's life… I have everything ready but I must stay and help here for a few more days… Where are you heading at?

- East…

- I'm going east too… more coincidences then…

- Maybe it's a sign of some kind…

- A sign telling us what?

- Oh, I don't know… maybe we should travel together? I'll travel by bus but I can arrange it at any time…

- Oh I have a car I'll be travelling with…

- Oh, you own car?

- No, it's not mine… I don't really need one… it's my sister's but she's on a trip the last three months and she lets me use it…

He looks amazed with her:

- So, you think we could travel together?

- We could, travel together…, John gets happy, But I don't know if we should…, now he is not happy, it's the first time we meet each other and… I believe one should love all people but of course he must take care of himself because even if he loves all people that doesn't mean that everybody loves him too…

John is again amazed and speachless.

She says:

- Oh, I'm sorry, I got carried away, I usually don't talk to people I don't know like that… I don't even talk to people I know like that…

John gets more thrilled with her:

- Yes I know, the word "love" often sounds strange to people… for me it was almost an unknown word just a few time ago… but know the only thing I care about is love.

- Yes, exactly! and she gets thrilled too.

John:

- You know, we have time to get to know each other a few days before we leave…

- Oh, I don't know…, John gets "dissapointed", …I think it's best if we meet straight away the day of our journey, we'll make a new acquaintance towards our destinations for our new lives…

John is really excited with her:

- …Our new life you said?

- Our new lives… but who knows it might turn to be a new life… for both of us…

- Ok, then let's arrange when we'll meet to leave for our new life…

- New lives…

- Yes, that's what I said…new life…

She laughs.

(Music: Is this love – Bob Marley).

Customers enter. They don't pay attention to anything around them. They arrange their schedule.

***

In the car. She's driving. They talk, laugh and look really happy.

***

(Music fades out)

She makes a stop:

- Do you mind if we stop here for a while?

- It's like you're reading my mind… I was just about to tell you to make a stop here!

They go outside. They get to the beach.

She says:

- Oh, it's so beautiful…

They sit in silence and admire the sea.

Then she says:

- It's strange… all this life that exists in the sea, all these strange and funny creatures. I have seen pictures of very strange and at the same truly beautiful fishes, they have forms that I couldn't perceive even with my wildest imagination… and not only fishes but plenty forms of life… God's creation is amazing… and we take everything for granted…

- You know what else seems very strange and funny to me… we, humans, we have our nice lives at the land and then we decide to take our clothes off, go into the sea and move our legs and arms so we can float! Because if we don't, we'll sink… and we'll be drowned because we're not made up for existing in the sea… and yet, we become one with it as we swim…

- And of course this swimming thing is also very amusing and relaxing…, and she gets up and pulls him up too, and why should we take our clothes off?… Come on…

She takes him to the sea and they swim.

***

They're again in the car.

John:

- You can stop right there… yes, here we are.

She stops. They look at each other.

John:

- I've never felt with anyone before, the way I feel with you, neither man nor woman…

- It may sound silly but it's like we're the missing part of each other…

They look at each other.

She says:

- But I think it's good to take this slow… start as friends, get to know each other…

- Yes, a true friendship must be the foundation of our future new lives…

- New life you mean…

- Yes that's what I said, new…, she stares at him, life…

They smile and hug each other.

John:

- So… you've seen where I live…

- Yes, I'll come and see you in a week, I don't think it should take more than half an hour with the car…

- So you think we'll need a car? …to see each other…

Both of them:

- Nah!

She says:

- I don't really like cars.

- Neither do I… don't worry we'll work it out…

- Yeah, maybe we'll get bikes…

- Yes, it will be a very good exercise… together we'll do many things…

- Yeah! I liked what you said… together we'll be working everything out…

They hug again.

John:

- Ok, have a nice journey to your home and thanks for getting me here…

- Bye.

- Bye.

John is leaving but then turns back again when she's about to speak too, so they say together:

- I'll call you.

They both laugh.

She says:

- Ok, we'll call each other, all right… goodbye then…

- Goodbye.

***

He goes to the front door with a few stuff he carries on. He knocks.

His mother opens:

- John! What a nice surprise!, and she hugs him.

- Hey mom!

Upon entering she looks at him:

- Is everything all right John? How come this sudden visit… and so soon from your last one… you only come twice a year… what's going on? They chase you or something?, she looks a little worried.

- Mom, I never did all these terrible things they say I did… it was the demon, it wasn't me… you got to believe me!

She looks at him questioningly.

They sit.

John:

- Come on mom, I just missed you and I thought of visiting you… though this visit might last a little longer…

- You know we're always happy to have you here, the longer the better…

- But I don't want to be a burden for you… I was thinking of staying at the guest-house…

- Oh John, we have talked about this… you can have this place only if you want to use it as your permanent residence, that's the only way you will take care of it…

John looks at her.

She thinks over this a little and says:

- Oh John, I can't believe this… you're coming back… and all this time you didn't call I was thinking that you were becoming more distant…, his mother looks moved.

- Oh, I'm sorry mom, I had a lot of things I had to clear out, that's why I didn't call… some of these were that I got tired of the city's air and that I missed you…

She hugs him:

- Your father will be so happy!

- You think?

- Oh, he might not say that much about your life but I know he believed you weren't happy and that was grieving him a lot.

- Now I'm happy mom, I'm truly happy…

***

John and his brother get two chairs to sit outside John's new house.

John:

- Thanks for helping me tidying this place up.

- Don't even mention it… but that's the only stuff you got?

- I have a few more that the guys are bringing next week but I gave away most of them…

They sit.

His brother:

- …You look changed …you look like someone who has made a discovery… I don't know how else to put it… you look like someone who knows something very important…

- I found a way to live each day as it would be my last…remember?

His brother nods "yes":

- …And how can you do that… by living dangerously?

- Oh, no, no, the way to live each day as it would be my last…, he stops for a while as he sees his father looking at them from a window with a smile of understanding, John smiles back and waves at him, is only through love… *conscious love*.

- "Conscious love"?.

- God's love… For example… you think God loves a sinner less than a saint? Of course not… He loves both equall, the only difference is that the sinner doesn't respond to God's love so he is unhappy while the saint responds to God's love by trying he himself to be love…

His brother repeats thoughtfully:

- Conscious love… God's love…

***

John is at his new house and makes a phone call:

- Hey Kate… How are you?… I'm glad you're ok… I couldn't be better… You got the books I've sent you?… oh really… you're on your way to discover the wisdom… I'm really glad for you… I knew you had it in you… the desire for love and happiness… ok, you too, we'll talk again, bye.

He hangs up the phone looking happy and filled with love.

***

He gets outside of his new house.

At the same time his friends arriving.

Matthew:

- There he is… coming from his newly obtained kingdom…

- Oh, hey guys!, he hugs every one of them.

Mark:

- This place is wonderful! …How come you didn't stay here earlier?

John:

- I was blinded by the city lights…

Matthew:

- Yeah… we were talking about moving to the country too, none of us is really much of a city-person.

Mark nods in agreement and Luke goes and looks at a tree as if he wants to climb it.

They all sit and John's family is coming too. Then John sees Her standing and watching them.

***

He goes to her. They look at each other and it's like the first time they met.

- Hey!

- Hey!

They hug.

She says:

- I see you have a 'friends and family' gathering.

- Oh, do you mind? I sould have told you but I-

- Don't worry, I don't mind at all… on the contrary, I know I will love the people you love… so I really want to meet them, I really appreciate it you invited me at your gathering…

He is amazed with her and speechless.

She says:

- And I like surprises… they keep you…

- Awake!

- Yes, exactly! …come on let's meet your beloved ones.

They go to the others.

They all look truly happy with love all around and inside them.

(Music: Jah is the way – Israel Vibration)

THE END

***

Epilogue

Conscious Love… God's Love:

"He maketh His sun to rise on the evil and on the good,

and sendeth rain on the just and on the unjust" (Mathew 5:45).